BIG BAD
WOLF'S
YOM KiPPUR

by David Sherrin

illustrated by Martín Morón

APPLES & HONEY PRESS

To my Big Bear, Medium Bear, and Little Bear. May you always share your porridge with those in need. —D.S.

To the little raccoon that lives in our hearts and can see the best in everyone. —M.M.

Apples & Honey Press
An Imprint of Behrman House Publishers
Millburn, New Jersey 07041
www.applesandhoneypress.com

ISBN 978-1-68115-606-4

Library of Congress Cataloging-in-Publication Data
Names: Sherrin, David, author. | Morón, Martín, illustrator.
Title: Big Bad Wolf's Yom Kippur / by David Sherrin; illustrated by Martín Morón.
Other titles: Little Red Riding Hood. English.
Description: Millburn, NJ : Apples & Honey Press, [2023] | Summary: "In this fractured fairytale, Wolf learns the value of kindness on Yom Kippur"-- Provided by publisher.
Identifiers: LCCN 2022019124 | ISBN 9781681156064 (hardcover)
Subjects: CYAC: Wolves--Fiction. | Yom Kippur--Fiction. | Fairy tales. lcgft | LCGFT: Picture books.
Classification: LCC PZ7.1.S5156 Bi 2023 | DDC [E]--dc23
LC record available at https://lccn.loc.gov/2022019124

Art Direction by Ann Koffsky
Design by Alexandra N. Segal
Edited by Alef Davis
Printed in China

9 8 7 6 5 4 3 2 1
0823/B2351/A6

It was just a regular morning
for the Big Bad Wolf . . . time
to get ready for a day full
of bad.

He heard a knock at the door.
Perhaps it was a grandmother.
He could cross one thing
off his list while having her
for breakfast.

But it was Raccoon.
"Wolf! I'm sorry for rummaging
through your garbage."

"I don't want my garbage anyway,"
Wolf grumbled. "What's gotten into you?"

"It's Yom Kippur, so I'm asking for forgiveness,"
Raccoon said. "I'm also going to synagogue.
Why don't you join me?"

Seeing all his neighbors in one place wasn't a
terrible idea. It would be like a lunch buffet for
a big hungry wolf.

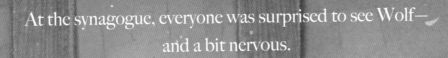

At the synagogue, everyone was surprised to see Wolf—
and a bit nervous.

But Rabbi Dov gave him a big bear hug.
"*Shanah tovah*, Wolf! What a joy to see you here!"
This hug feels cozy, thought Wolf. Then he remembered . . .
a Big Bad Wolf doesn't like hugs.

Cantor Zipporah led the animals in song,
her chirps floating into the air like butterflies.

Wolf almost howled along,
but then he remembered...
a Big Bad Wolf doesn't sing.

Rabbi Dov talked about how the leaves change color each fall, and how everyone in the forest could also become a little better and brighter.

Wrapped up in the peaceful moment, Wolf wondered: Could I become better and brighter?

Then he remembered...
a Big Bad Wolf doesn't change.
So after services he walked through
the forest toward home,
alone as always.

Then he saw a girl in a red riding hood.
"Where are you off to, little girl?"

"My Granny isn't feeling well, so I'm bringing her an apple cake," Little Red Riding Hood said. "But I can't find her cottage."

Wolf could snatch the yummy treat and run. Even better: he could race ahead and devour that helpless granny. His eyes widened, and he licked his lips.

"Oh my! What big teeth you have!" Little Red Riding Hood said.

Wolf grabbed the apple cake. But before he could wolf it down,
it slipped from his paws.

"Oh no!" said Little Red Riding Hood.

He noticed the way her red hood matched the autumn leaves.

Wolf felt his belly twist and turn...
and it wasn't even from hunger. He
almost said "Sorry." But he knew a
Big Bad Wolf doesn't say sorry.
"I know the cottage," he said instead.
"I'll take you there."

At the cottage, Granny gave
Little Red Riding Hood a kiss.

"*Mamaleh*, you brought Wolf!
How nice to have another guest!"
Then she wrapped him up in a hug
as tight as an apple strudel.

That reminded Wolf of the warm
apple cake he had dropped.

"We'll make you something to eat," he said.

"Oh, I don't eat on Yom Kippur!" said Granny.
"I'm fasting."

"If you're sick, you have to eat,"
insisted Little Red Riding Hood.
"Even on Yom Kippur."

Wolf and Little Red Riding Hood
served granny from a steaming pot of soup.
While she ate, Wolf's tummy growled.
But he wanted to leave every
drop for the sick granny.

"Come back anytime!" she said.
Wolf felt a strange warmth in his chest
and a funny beat in his heart.

On his way home, Wolf noticed three houses: one of straw, one of sticks, and one of brick. He also saw a potential three-course meal. His mouth began to water. The sunlight glinted off his sharp white teeth.
(He may have been a bad wolf, but he was a careful brusher.)

The plump, juicy owners raced inside . . .

and slammed the doors.

Just then, the wind blew a flurry of leaves around
the straw house. The walls began to sway.

"Little Pig! Little Pig! Let me in!" called Wolf.

"Not by the hairs on my chinny chin chin!"
the Little Pig yelled.

"I'm just worried about your house!" Wolf said.
"It will blow over in the lightest storm."

And he showed her. Wolf huffed and puffed, and the straw house swayed back and forth.

Then he told Little Pig how to pack the straw into tight bales to make the house sturdier.

"Now let's see about the stick house," Wolf said. He huffed and puffed, and the house began to sway.

"You should use thicker wood," Wolf recommended.

When he huffed and puffed at the
brick house, it didn't sway one inch.
This house would be just fine.

"Thank you for all your help!" squeaked the Three
Little Pigs. Wolf felt his heart beating in that funny
way again. *I need to see a doctor*, he thought.

As he walked home, his belly howled
as if there were a full moon. *The rabbi
got it all wrong*, he thought.
A wolf couldn't change.

He was alone, thinking about food as always.
A shofar blasted in the distance. Yom Kippur was over.

Then he heard a knock.

"*Shanah tovah!*" squealed the Three Little Pigs.
"You were such a great helper!"

"And cooking partner!"
Little Red Riding Hood added.

"I'm sorry for slamming the door
on you, Raccoon. And for taking
your apple cake, Little Red. And
for scaring you, Little Piggies."

"We forgive you, my friend,"
said Raccoon.

Helper. Partner. Friend.

Thinking about those words made Wolf's heart flutter and his chest get warm again. But this time he didn't mind at all.

He knew this was exactly how a Big Good Wolf should feel on Yom Kippur.

Dear Friends,

Can a big BAD wolf become a big GOOD wolf?

In this story, Wolf realizes that he has made mistakes and decides to change and become a "better and brighter" wolf, even though it's hard. In Jewish tradition, we call this *t'shuvah*, which means returning to our best selves.

The holiday of Yom Kippur is the perfect opportunity to think about ways we can be our best and brightest selves, just as Wolf did. It's a day to take the time to say sorry to those we may have hurt and figure out ways to give a helping hand (or paw) to others.

When was the last time you said "I'm sorry" to someone? Was it hard to do? How did you feel before you said it? How did you feel afterward?

What can you do on Yom Kippur and every day to be your best and brightest self?

Shalom,

David